Glamorous Glasses

Barbara Johansen Newman

BOYDS MILLS PRESS

Honesdale, Pennsylvania

Boyds Mills Press, Inc.
815 Church Street
Honesdale, Pennsylvania 18431
Printed in China

ISBN: 978-1-59078-878-3
Library of Congress Control Number: 2012934129

First edition
Designed by Barbara Grzeslo
Production by Margaret Mosomillo
The text of this book is set in Galahad.
The display type is hand lettered by Barbara Johansen Newman.
The illustrations are done in conventional and digital mixed media.

10 9 8 7 6 5 4 3 2 1

For my mother, who patiently took me to countless eye doctors in my quest to finagle a pair of glasses when I didn't need them   —BJN

PS: Mom, I finally need them!

Joanie

Me

Mom

Aunt → Tessie

I have a best cousin named Joanie. Mom has a best sister named Tessie. We are all best friends, and we do *everything* together.

One day Mom said, "Bobbie, your cousin Joanie needs glasses. She's not very happy about it, so we're going to help her pick out a pair."

I think we'd walked past the eyeglasses store before.
But I'd never really noticed it—until now. In the window,
there were all kinds of glasses. The beautiful colors and
shapes made my eyes happy. And you know what?

Inside, there were even *more* glasses.

Zillions of beautiful glasses!

Joanie tried on lots of styles. The glasses she liked best were blue with specks of gold. I thought she looked very glamorous.

"I *guess* this is the pair I want," she said.

I tried on lots of styles. The glasses I liked best had red
and white stripes. I looked even more glamorous.
"This is definitely the pair *I* want!" I said.

"Barbara Louise," my mother said. "You do not need glasses."

"I *do* need them," I
said. "I need them to look
glamorous."

Nope. No glasses and no
looking glamorous for me.

After that, I saw eyeglasses everywhere! Big ones, little ones, round ones, square ones. Glasses with jewels and glasses in crayon colors. I even saw glasses that had glasses! It seemed *everybody* had glamorous glasses. Everybody but me.

Then one day in school, I got an idea. . . .

I missed the ball in gym.

I pretended I couldn't see the blackboard.

I tripped over kids during reading time.

I was not surprised when my teacher called my mom. "I think Bobbie may need glasses," she said. *Goody!* I thought. *Back to the eyeglasses store.*

Nope! Straight to the eye doctor.
"Young lady, you have perfect vision," the doctor said.
"Come back and see me when you're about forty years old."
My mother thought that was very funny.

When we got home, Joanie and Aunt Tessie came over so we could walk into town for some shopping. Joanie was wearing her new glasses. Her glamorous, new blue glasses that turned up at the ends like a smiley mouth.

"Are Bobbie's eyes okay?" Aunt Tessie asked. "Does she need glasses?"

"Bobbie's eyes are just fine," Mom said. "She does not need glasses."

"You are so lucky," said Joanie. "Wearing glasses makes me feel different. I don't like the way I look. I wish I didn't have to wear them."

I couldn't believe my ears. I'd give *anything* to wear glasses like Joanie's. That's when I got another idea. . . .

"Listen, Joanie," I whispered. "While our moms are trying on dresses today, we can go get some candy. I'll wear your new glasses, and you can carry my new pocketbook. We'll both look very glamorous."

"I like that idea!" said Joanie.

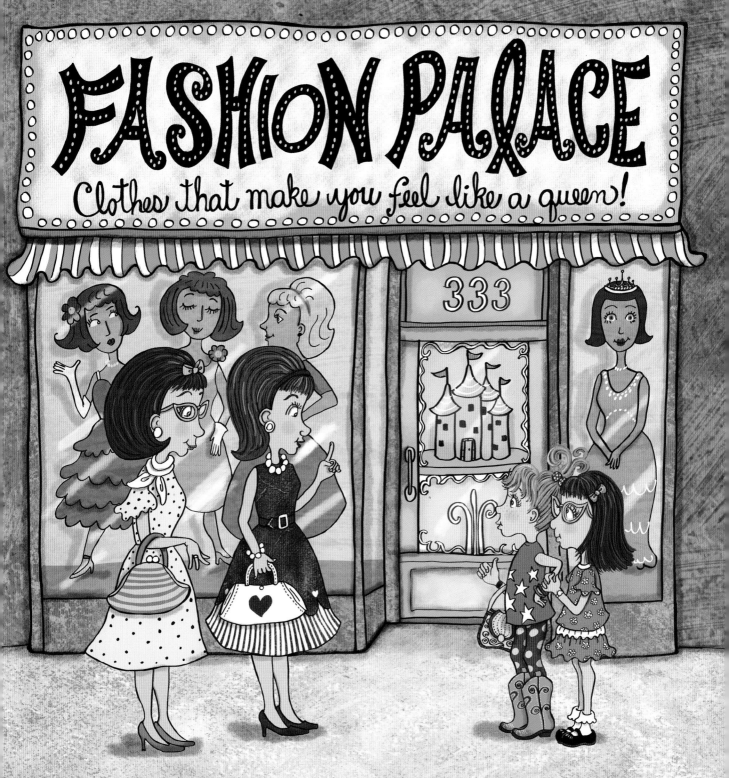

We all walked into town. When Mom and Aunt Tessie
headed into Fashion Palace, I said, "Is it okay if we go to
Sophie's Sweet Shoppe for some candy?"
"Yes," they said, "but don't be too long."

As soon as the door closed behind them, I put Joanie's glasses on my face, and Joanie put my pocketbook on her arm. We marched down the street wearing big smiles. Glamorous girls smiled back at us from store windows.

"Everything is kind of blurry," Joanie said. "I can't see so well."

"Me, neither," I said. "The sidewalk looks crooked."

Somehow, we made it to Sophie's. Joanie pointed to
a big jar of candy. "I'd like ten of those, please," she said.
I pointed to a different jar. "I'd like ten of those,
please," I said.

On the way back to Fashion Palace, we held onto each other. But I still bumped into a lady with groceries.

"Watch where you're walking!" she told me.

Joanie stepped on a poodle's paw.

Yip, yip, yipe! he barked. I think that meant "Look where you're going!" in poodle talk.

We watched and we looked. Even so, we didn't see a big crack in the sidewalk. We both tripped—and the glasses went flying off my face and disappeared.

We hunted high and low. Then I saw something blue
and shiny: Joanie's glasses!

She put them right on. "You know what?" she said. "I like seeing where I'm going much more than I *don't* like wearing my glasses."

"You know what else?" I said. "I like seeing where I'm going much more than I *do* like wearing your glasses."

That made us smile.

"Let's celebrate with some candy," I said.

"I like that idea!" Joanie said. She popped a piece into her mouth, and I popped one into mine.

"Eeew!" she said. "I couldn't see what I was pointing to at Sophie's. I bought gummy bugs instead of sour bears."

"Blech!" I said. "I did the same thing. Only I bought malted mints instead of fireballs."

That made us giggle.

Mom and Aunt Tessie came out of Fashion Palace. "What's so funny, cousins?" they asked.

We didn't tell. But on the way home, something amazing happened. Something that made us really laugh.

YARD
SALE

COOKIES

You know what? Now we're *both* really glamorous!